Seriously Silly Stories

BILLY BEAST

Compass Point Books
3109 West 50th Street, #115
Minneapolis, MN 55410

Visit Compass Point Books on the Internet at *www.compasspointbooks.com*
or e-mail your request to *custserv@compasspointbooks.com*

Library of Congress Cataloging-in-Publication Data
Anholt, Laurence.
  Billy Beast / by Laurence Anholt. Illustrated by Arthur Robins.
    p. cm. — (Seriously silly stories)
Summary: In this humorous version of "Beauty and the Beast," Billy Beast wonders if
the clean and proper Beauty will ever be the beast of his dreams.
ISBN 0-7565-0628-X (hardcover)
    [1. Fairy tales. 2. Humorous stories.] I. Title II. Series: Anholt, Laurence. Seriously
silly stories.
    PZ8.A577Bi 2004
    [E]—dc22   2003017949

For more information on *Billy Beast,* use FactHound
to track down Web sites related to this book.

1. Go to *www.compasspointbooks.com/facthound*
2. Type in this book ID: 075650628X
3. Click on the *Fetch It* button.

Your trusty FactHound will fetch the best Web sites for you!

About the Author
Laurence Anholt is one of the UK's leading authors. From his home in
Dorset, he has produced more than 80 books, which are published all
around the world. His Seriously Silly Stories have won numerous
awards, including the Smarties Gold Award for "Snow White and the
Seven Aliens."

About the Illustrator
Arthur Robins has illustrated more than 50 picture books, all of them
highly successful and popular titles, and is the illustrator for all the
Seriously Silly Stories. His energetic and fun-filled drawings have been
featured in countless magazines, advertisements, and animations. He
lives with his wife and two daughters in Surrey, England.

First published in Great Britain by Orchard Books, 96 Leonard Street, London EC2A 4XD

Text © Laurence Anholt 1996/Illustrations © Arthur Robins 1996

Printed in the United States of America.

Seriously Silly Stories

BILLY BEAST

Written by Laurence Anholt
Illustrated by Arthur Robins

COMPASS POINT BOOKS

Minneapolis, Minnesota

4

Betty and Benjamin Beast were very proud of their castle.

They thought it was the most wonderful building for miles around. It had taken them years to get it just right with lovely green moldy walls and black puddles in the corridors.

6

There were damp, dark bedrooms with
snails on the pillows and smelly cellars, too.

On weekends, you would always find
Benjamin up a stepladder whistling happily
as he hung new cobwebs in corners or
painted fresh mud on the ceilings.

And when their beastly friends came for dinner, it was hard not to show off the new kitchen with its sweet little scampering cockroaches in all the cupboards, and hot and cold running slime in the taps.

There was only one thing that Betty and Benjamin were more proud of than their home, and that was their fine young son, Billy Beast.

13

They loved Billy more than words can say,
and the truth is, Billy was a little spoiled.

They were always giving him some little treat or other—an enormous pet toad in a box, or as much crunchy termite ice cream as a beastly boy could eat, which wasn't very good for him.

Billy always had the best of everything—even private belching lessons after Beastie School.

By the time he was sixteen, Billy had grown into a fine-looking beast. He was tall and strong with plenty of fleas in his hair and the sharpest brown teeth a beast could wish for.

The truth was, there wasn't a girl beast around who wasn't in love with young Billy, with those twinkling yellow eyes and that cute way he had of wiping his snout with the hairs on the back of his hand— who could resist?

18

But as far as Benjamin and Betty were concerned, it would have to be a very special girl beast who could be disgusting enough to marry their son.

So the three of them just carried on living happily together from day to day.

Billy and his toad practiced their burping, and everyone who met the Beast family thought they were the luckiest, smelliest, most horribly beautiful family they had ever met.

Then one morning, Benjamin and Betty went out gathering tadpoles for lunch, leaving young Billy playing quietly with his toad in his bedroom.

Billy heard a noise outside. When he looked out of his window, he saw an old man wandering about in their beautiful weedy garden. He had tied his horse to the tree, and he was busy STEALING BETTY'S PRIZE-WINNING PRICKLY ROSES!

"Hey! What do you think you're doing?" shouted Billy. "This is a private castle, you know. My mom will eat you if she catches you here."

When the man looked up at the castle
and saw young Billy Beast all hairy and
horrid with a big toad sitting on his head,
he was absolutely TERRIFIED.

"Oh p-please don't eat me, Mr. Beast," he stammered. "I got lost and . . . and I promised my beautiful daughter I would bring her a red rose and . . ."

"Well, not from our garden, pal!" snorted Billy.

The man was so frightened, he promised that he would send his daughter, Beauty, to marry Billy if he was allowed to go free.

"All right," Billy agreed, "but she'd better come soon or my dad will be after you, too."

"I . . . I'll send her right away," said the poor man, jumping onto his horse.

"And she'd better be as beautiful as you say," Billy called after him.

"Oh yes, oh yes she is," shouted the man riding away as fast as he could. "There's nothing in the world more beautiful than my daughter."

"What? More beautiful than my toad?" called Billy. But the man was already out of sight.

When Betty and Benjamin came home, Billy told them the whole story. "I'm going to be married," he grunted happily, "to the most beautiful girl in the world—the man said there's nothing in the world more beautiful than Beauty."

Betty and Benjamin were very pleased to think of their son married to the most beautiful girl in the world, although they found it hard to believe that anyone could be quite as good-looking as their Billy.

Early the next morning, Beauty arrived. Billy saw her horse coming up the hill toward the castle.

He quickly ran to the mirror to make
sure his teeth were nice and black, and he
checked that his breath was good and
smelly. He splashed a little skunk juice
under his arms—then he ran to the door to
meet his bride.

Billy was very excited. As the doorbell rang, he twisted his face into the most beautifully disgusting shape that he could manage, then pulled open the door.

When Beauty saw Billy, she almost
fainted on the spot. Billy could understand
that, because his handsome looks often
made girls feel weak in the knees.

What he couldn't understand was that Beauty wasn't beautiful! In fact, she looked just like an ordinary GIRL!

She was hardly hairy at all, except on her head. And her TEETH—they were all sort of white and shiny!

She had a horrid pink NOSE where her snout should be and little FINGERS instead of nice claws. UGH! It was DIS-GUSTING!

"I bet she hasn't even got a hairy chest," thought Billy in dismay.

Betty and Benjamin were also disappointed, but they tried not to show it.

The poor girl had come a long way to marry their son, and she seemed upset, too.

"I'm sure she will look better once we get rid of that nasty white dress and pop her into a nice, sloppy, mud bath," said Betty kindly.

"And she'll probably get hairier as she gets older," suggested Benjamin. "Perhaps she hasn't been eating a healthy diet—I suppose she's hungry now after that long journey. Let's start her off with a lovely bowl of warm earwax and slug juice."

So Betty and Benjamin set about trying to make Beauty a little more beastly, and Billy went into the garden with his toad and sulked.

After a few days, Beauty began to get used to living with the Beasts, and Billy had to admit that she was looking a little better; at least she was getting smellier.

But then Beauty would go and spoil it all by doing something revolting like washing her hands before a meal or combing her hair, and everyone realized that no matter how they tried, Beauty would never be truly disgusting.

Billy promised his parents that he would try to get along with her, although he swore he would never marry her. He patiently taught her to burp nicely and to drool, but she was slow to learn.

Then, one morning in the garden, something horrid happened. Billy had just allowed Beauty to play with his toad when she turned around and TRIED TO KISS HIM!

With those white teeth and rosy lips, it almost made poor Billy sick just thinking about it! He wiped his mouth and jumped away.

Beauty began to cry, "I can't help it!" she wailed. "I can't help looking like this. Of course I would like to be hairy and horrid like you. But couldn't you try to love me for what I am instead of the way I look."

Billy was really a kind-hearted beast. He began to feel sorry for Beauty. He saw that she was right. It doesn't really matter what you look like, it is the person inside that counts.

Before he knew what he was doing, Billy had put down his toad and taken Beauty into his hairy arms, he put his snout close to her little head and . . . SMACK!

He kissed her tiny snubby nose.

Right before Billy's yellow eyes, Beauty
began to change! She grew hairier and
hairier. Her teeth grew brown and longer.
Her fingers turned into beautiful claws!

At last she stood before him—a truly
wonderful beastie girl with the most
gorgeous damp snout Billy had ever seen
and a delightful smell of old socks and
kangaroo sweat.

Beauty explained that the man who had stolen the roses was not her father, but a wicked wizard who had cast a spell on her.

She would lose her beastly looks until the day someone like Billy was kind enough to kiss her and break the spell.

Billy was so happy, he didn't know what to say. He just drooled a little. And the beastly couple skipped happily up the steps of the castle, claw in claw, burping excitedly to each other.

And they were all disgustingly happy
for the rest of their beastly lives.